Life in the Rain Forest

CAPSTONE PRESS
a capstone imprint

Sarah Levete

First Facts is published by Capstone Press, a Capstone imprint,
151 Good Counsel Drive, P.O. Box 669, Mankato, Minnesota 56002.
www.capstonepub.com

First published in 2010 by A&C Black Publishers Limited, 36 Soho Square, London W1D 3QY
www.acblack.com

Produced for A&C Black by Calcium. www.calciumcreative.co.uk

Printed in China

042010
005769ACS11

Library of Congress Cataloging-in-Publication Data
Levete, Sarah
Life in the rain forest / by Sarah Levete.
p. cm. — (First Facts, the big picture)
Includes bibliographical references and index.
ISBN 978-1-4296-5525-5 (library binding)
ISBN 978-1-4296-5526-2 (paperback)
1. Rain forests—Juvenile literature. I. Title. II. Series.

QH86.G357 2011
578.734—dc22 2010015739

Acknowledgements

The publishers would like to thank the following for their kind permission to reproduce their photographs:

Cover: Shutterstock: Tom C Amon (front), Ethylalkohol (back). **Pages:** Fotolia: Roman Shiyanov 19; Shutterstock: Galyna Andrushko 6-7, Anyka 6-7, Matthew Cole 16, Ethylalkohol 14, Frontpage 20-21, Eric Gevaert 1, 8, Eric Isselée 11, Kkaplin 9, 24, Timur Kulgarin 13, Michael Lynch 17, Steve Mann 8-9, Antonio Jorge Nunes 4-5, 16-17, Dr. Morley Read 2-3, 15, 18-19, 22-23, Rsfatt 3, Chai Kian Shin 5, Szefei 14-15, Charles Taylor 20-21, Wouter Tolenaars 10-11, Tonobalaguerf 12-13, Worldswildlifewonders 10.

Contents

This green, leafy place is bursting with tall trees, plants, and animals.

Sunshine and rain

Rain forests grow in places where there is a lot of rain and sunshine.

Hot and wet

Gobble gobble

Some plants eat animals in rain forests. The **pitcher plant** traps animals and insects. Then it eats them!

A pitcher plant can grow as tall as a house.

Lots of Rain

It is hot in the rain forest. It rains most of the time, but it is sunny too.

No sun below

Rain forest trees are very tall. Their huge leaves catch the sun so it is dark on the ground.

Many rain forest animals like the rain.

Raining again

Raindrops fall onto rain forest leaves. They dry in the sun, then rise back into the air. Later, they fall back down again as raindrops.

Drip, drop

Living Here

Animals and plants live in every part of the rain forest, from the tree tops to bushes on the ground.

Staying alive

The rain forest gives animals and plants food, water, and a place to live. Without these things, animals and plants die.

Monkeys live in rain forests.

Big and smelly

Make sure you don't get too close to the raffelesia plant. It is the biggest plant in the world—and it stinks of rotten meat. Disgusting!

Frog Forest

Frogs are everywhere in the rain forest. They jump around the forest floor, and climb up trees.

Dark and bright

Some frogs are dark to help them hide in the trees. Others are very colorful. The frog's bright colors warn others that it is **poisonous**.

Hands off!

Poisonous skin

Don't touch!

Poison dart frogs are **deadly**. There is enough poison in their skin to kill a big animal, such as a **jaguar**.

This tree frog uses sticky pads on its feet to climb up trees.

Bird World

Lots and lots of different birds live in rain forests. They make the rain forest colorful and noisy!

Nut cracker

The toucan likes to eat fruit and nuts. When it eats fruit, the **seeds** drop to the ground and grow into new trees.

Bee hummingbirds fly among rain forest trees.

Keep flapping

Super small

The bee hummingbird is so small it can sit on the tip of a pencil. It flaps its tiny wings up to 200 times a second.

Creepy Crawlies!

From beautiful butterflies to huge spiders, rain forests are full of creepy crawlies and insects.

Cleaning up

Dead animals and plants lie on the rain forest ground. They are eaten by beetles and **cockroaches**.

Killer bug

The assassin bug is small but deadly. It jumps on passing insects, then sucks out their insides. Horrible!

Cockroaches eat any dead animals lying around.

Staying Alive

It's not easy for animals in the rain forest. But they have amazing ways of staying alive.

Ssssss

If the king cobra snake is frightened, it will attack. It rises up until it is as tall as a human man—then bites!

One bite from a king cobra can be deadly.

Vampires

Vampire bats drink blood to stay alive. They even drink human blood! They bite their prey, then lick its blood.

Special Plants

Some of the things we use every day are made from rain forest plants.

Chocolate forest

Soap, bubble gum, and chocolate are just some of the things made from plants that grow in the rain forest.

Keeping well

People who live in rain forests make medicines from rain forest plants. Many of our medicines are made from these plants too.

Rain forest people know which plants are safe to use as medicines.

In Danger

Half of the world's animals and plants live in rain forests. But people are chopping down rain forest trees for wood and to build on the land.

Lost forever

Every second, an area of rain forest the size of a soccer field is chopped down.

Orangutans and other animals will die out if their rain forest trees are cut down.

You can help

Help to save the rain forests by:

- Telling people about the dangers to rain forests.
- Raising money for a **charity** that helps rain forests.

Glossary

charity group of people who try to help people, animals, or places that are in danger

cockroaches beetles that feed on rubbish and rotting food

deadly can kill

jaguar big cat that lives in rain forests

pitcher plant plant that has a juglike part into which animals fall or crawl. Once the animal is inside, the plant eats it.

poisonous makes you very ill or kills you if it gets inside your body

seeds small parts of plants that can grow into a new plant

Further Reading

FactHound offers a safe, fun way to find Internet sites related to this book. All of the sites on FactHound have been researched by our staff.

Here's all you do:

Visit www.facthound.com

FactHound will fetch the best sites for you!

Books

Who Lives in a Wet, Wild Rain Forest by Rachel Lynette, PowerKids Press (2011).

Life in a Rain Forest by Lorien Kite, Gareth Stevens (2010).

Index